M116k

Kirsty Knows Best

by Annalena McAfee
illustrated by Anthony Browne

🐎 ALFRED A. KNOPF · NEW YORK

THIS IS A BORZOI BOOK PUBLISHED BY ALFRED A. KNOPF, INC.

Text copyright © 1987 by Annalena McAfee. Illustrations copyright © 1987 by Anthony Browne. All rights reserved under International and Pan-American Copyright Conventions. Published in the United States by Alfred A. Knopf, Inc., New York, and simultaneously in Canada by Random House of Canada Limited, Toronto. Distributed by Random House, Inc., New York. Originally published in Great Britain by Julia MacRae Books, London. Manufactured in Italy
Library of Congress Cataloging-in-Publication Data: McAfee, Annalena. Kirsty knows best. Summary: A child's day-dreams turn her ordinary life into a much more interesting one. [1. Imagination—Fiction. 2. Stories in rhyme] I. Browne, Anthony. II. Title. PZ7.M4782Ki 1987 [E] 87-3359 ISBN 0-394-89478-2 ISBN 0-394-99478-7 (lib. bdg.)
1 3 5 7 9 10 8 6 4 2

rincess Kirsty stirs in bed
And tries to plan the day ahead.
Should she rush to the royal stables?
Or help the cook lay breakfast tables?
Should she joke with the royal fool?
Or stop by at the palace school?
Should she play with her favorite toys?
But, hark! What's that horrendous noise?

"Kirsty! *Kirsty!* Come down and have your breakfast or you'll be late for school."
Mom's voice was shriller than an alarm clock.
Shivering, Kirsty left her warm bed and dressed for school.

"Stop your daydreaming," said Mrs. Little.
"How many times do I have to tell you, you'll be
late for school if you don't hurry up!"
But Kirsty's mind was elsewhere....

ost people wait till Christmas
For a feast as good as this.
But every day in Kirsty's house
There's a meal too good to miss.
With candies, cakes, and pink ice cream,
And other tempting food,
There are funny hats and paper chains
To put you in the mood.
It's just the thing to get you up
Before you start the day.
Breakfast time is party time
When Kirsty has her way.

Although Kirsty had a long walk to school,
she was never bored.

Sometimes Nora Nelson, the school bully, leaned out of the window of her mother's car and sneered, "Get a move on, slowpoke, or you'll be late for school again."
But Kirsty wasn't listening....

s far as modes of transport go
A horse is quite divine,
And coaches have a special charm,
Sedan chairs, too, are fine.
But Kirsty's favorite is quite plain;
Instead of horse, or coach, or train,
To get round town she does adore her
Little rickshaw pulled by Nora.

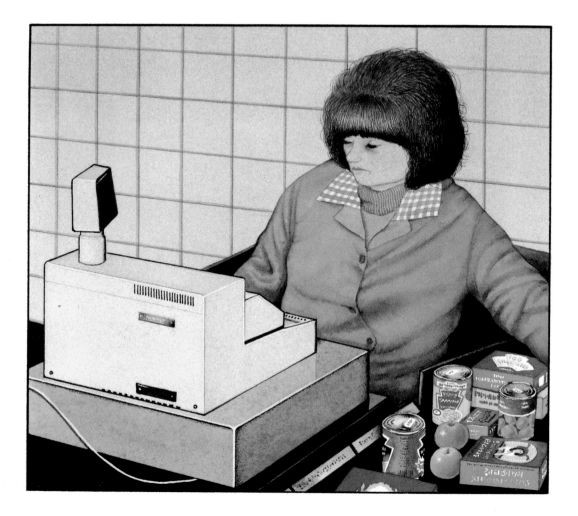

After Kirsty had gone to school, her mom went to work in a local supermarket.

Mrs. Little said the only fun she ever had was
her monthly visit to town for a shampoo and set.
But Kirsty knew better....

The crowds are hushed,
The band strikes up,
Then everybody cheers
As, dressed in glittering finery,
The special guest appears.
Her fame has spread
Throughout the world;
They come from near and far,
To hear the golden singing of
Joyce Little, superstar.

Kirsty's dad, Reg, didn't have to get up early every morning. He didn't have a job.

In the evenings, when Kirsty and her mom were
home, he liked to putter around in the toolshed.
At least that's what he said he did.
But Kirsty knew better....

In his secret lab in the garden shed,
He pushes the frontiers of science ahead.
His latest scheme set the town agog
When he unleashed Fido the Flying Dog.
Not content with this small operation,
He's set his heart on world domination.

Days at Kingly School seemed endless.
All the children, especially Nora, thought that
playtime was too short and lessons too long.
But not Kirsty.

The teacher droned on and on.
Kirsty was far away....

"Kirsty! *Kirsty!* Repeat what I just said!"
But she never could.

At playtime Kirsty was always left out.
Nora made sure of that.
But Kirsty didn't mind.

One day Nora turned on Kirsty.
"You spend so much time daydreaming, you
look like a sleepwalker. Wake up!

"Wake up, wake up! Your mom's a drudge, your dad's a slob, and you're as dense as a jailyard fence."
But Kirsty wasn't upset. She knew better....

s nasty Nora sneers and puffs
The strangest thing takes place.
Her body swells, her eyes grow large
And dwarf her little face.

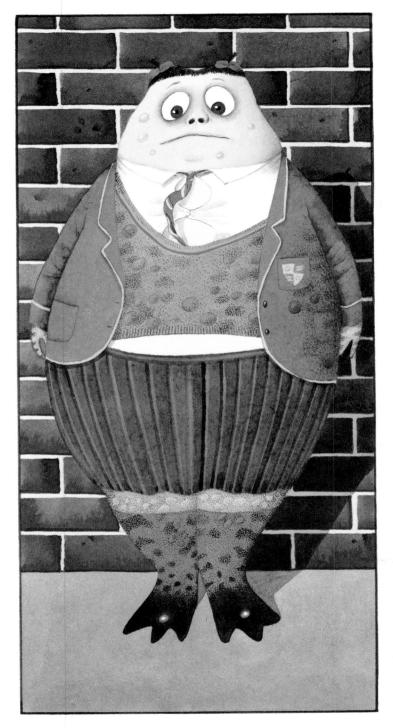

he turns bright green
And then is seen
To turn into a toad.
And everyone is open-mouthed
To see the toad…

But Kirsty knows better....